Good Times

ALL ABOUT THE SEASONS

Written by Kirsten Hall
Illustrated by Bev Luedecke

children's press®

A Division of Scholastic Inc.
New York Toronto London Auckland Sydney
Mexico City New Delhi Hong Kong
Danbury, Connecticut

About the Author

Kirsten Hall, formerly an early-childhood teacher,
is a children's book editor in New York City. She has been
writing books for children since she was thirteen years old
and now has over sixty titles in print.

About the Illustrator

Bev Luedecke enjoys life and nature in Colorado.
Her sparkling personality and artistic flair are reflected in her
creation of Beastieville, a world filled with lovable Beasties
that are sure to delight children of all ages.

Library of Congress Cataloging-in-Publication Data

Hall, Kirsten.
  Good times : all about the seasons / written by Kirsten Hall ; illustrated by Bev Luedecke.
    p. cm. — (Beastieville)
  Summary: On the first day of fall, the Beasties each proclaim which is their favorite season, and why.
  ISBN 0-516-23648-2 (lib. bdg.)   0-516-25518-5 (pbk.)
  [1. Seasons—Fiction. 2. Stories in rhyme.] I. Luedecke, Bev, ill. II. Title.
  PZ8.3.H146Goo 2004
  [E]—dc22
                          2004000109

A NOTE TO PARENTS AND TEACHERS

Welcome to the world of the Beasties, where learning is FUN. In each of the charming stories in this series, the Beasties deal with character traits that every child can identify with. Each story reinforces appropriate concept skills for kinder-gartners and first graders, while simultaneously encouraging problem-solving skills. Following are just a few of the ways that you can help children get the most from this delightful series.

Stories to be read and enjoyed

Encourage children to read the stories aloud. The rhyming verses make them fun to read. Then ask them to think about alternate solutions to some of the prob-lems that the Beasties have faced or to imagine alternative endings. Invite chil-dren to think about what they would have done if they were in the story and to recall similar things that have happened to them.

Activities reinforce the learning experience

The activities at the end of the books offer a way for children to put their new skills to work. They complement the story and are designed to help children develop specific skills and build confidence. Use these activities to reinforce skills. But don't stop there. Encourage children to find ways to build on these skills during the course of the day.

Learning opportunities are everywhere

Use this book as a starting point for talking about how we use reading skills or math or social studies concepts in everyday life. When we search for a phone number in the telephone book and scan names in alphabetical order or check a list, we are using reading skills. When we keep score at a baseball game or divide a class into even-numbered teams, we are using math.

The more you can help children see that the skills they are learning in school really do have a place in everyday life, the more they will think of learning as something that is part of their lives, not as a chore to be borne. Plus you will be sending the important message that learning is fun.

Madeline Boskey Olsen, Ph.D.
Developmental Psychologist

Bee-Bop

Puddles

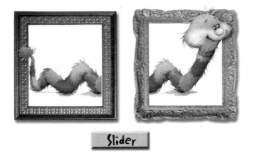

Slider

Wilbur

Pip & Zip

Flippet

Pooky

Mr. Rigby

Smudge

We're the Beasties

Toggles

It is Monday in September.
All the Beasties are in school.

Toggles points up at the window.
"Look outside! The leaves look cool!"

Mr. Rigby smiles at his class.
"It is the first day of fall!"

8

Leaves are blowing in the school yard.
Toggles says, "Look at them all!"

Then she claps her hands together.
She loves fall! She loves the trees.

10

She loves all the reds and yellows.
She loves all the leaves she sees.

Bee-Bop feels the same as Toggles.
"Toggles, I agree with you!

I miss school when it is summer.
When it's fall, our books are new!"

Smudge starts dreaming of the winter.
"I just love it when it snows!

I am good at making snowmen.
I like snowflakes on my nose!"

Slider also likes the winter.
"When it snows, I stay inside!

I love sleeping with my blanket.
I curl up inside and hide!"

Pooky does not like the winter.
She tells her friends, "I like spring!

That is when the birds are happy.
That is when they like to sing!"

Wilbur does not have a favorite.
"I do not like any one!

Do not ask me for a favorite.
Choosing seasons is not fun."

Flippet calls out, "I love summer!"
"Summer is the best for me!

It is hot, but I love swimming.
And I love my shady tree."

Zip and Pip agree with Flippet.
"We love summer, just like you!

We love going out for picnics.
We pack lunches made for two!"

Mr. Rigby looks at his class.
"I agree with each of you!

Every season can be special.
Now I know what we must do!"

Mr. Rigby grabs his jacket.
He has one more thing to say.

"I think we should go outside now.
Fall is a great time to play!"

SEASONS

1. How many seasons are there in a year?

2. How many Beasties like summertime the best?

3. How many paintings has Toggles made?

FAVORITES

1. What is your favorite season? Why?

2. What is your least favorite season? Why?

3. Why are we lucky to have different seasons?

WORD LIST

a	does	is	one	snowmen	winter
agree	dreaming	it	our	snows	with
all	each	it's	out	special	yard
also	every	jacket	outside	spring	yellows
am	fall	just	pack	starts	you
and	favorite	know	picnics	stay	Zip
any	feels	leaves	Pip	summer	
are	first	like	play	swimming	
as	Flippet	likes	points	tells	
ask	for	look	Pooky	that	
at	friends	looks	reds	the	
be	fun	love	Rigby	them	
Beasties	go	loves	same	then	
Bee-Bop	going	lunches	say	they	
best	good	made	says	thing	
birds	grabs	making	school	think	
blanket	great	me	season	time	
blowing	hands	miss	seasons	to	
books	happy	Monday	sees	together	
but	has	more	September	Toggles	
calls	have	Mr.	shady	tree	
can	he	must	she	trees	
choosing	her	my	should	two	
claps	hide	new	sing	up	
class	his	nose	sleeping	we	
cool	hot	not	Slider	what	
curl	I	now	smiles	when	
day	in	of	Smudge	Wilbur	
do	inside	on	snowflakes	window	